About Twins

By Shelley Rotner
and
Sheila M. Kelly

Photographs by
Shelley Rotner

A DK INK BOOK

DK PUBLISHING, INC.

For Parents

TWINS PUZZLE AND INTRIGUE everyone, and the increase in twin births in the past decade has added to our interest. The increase is explained by the fact that more women are taking fertility drugs and having children at an older age, when they are more likely to bear twins. At the same time, the scientific study of twins has increased, and researchers continue to find new ways in which twins differ from single-born children.

Twins are of special interest to researchers who study whether child rearing or genetics has more significance. Because they develop from a single egg that splits soon after conception, identical twins are of chief importance in these studies. Non-identical, or fraternal, twins de-

velop from two eggs. Studies done across the life span of twins show that both fraternal and identical twins share a unique bond.

While the similarities and differences between twins capture our attention, parents of twins have a special challenge in helping each one to develop a sense of unique individuality. This concern is expressed in the definition of twins provided by the American Medical Association in the *Encyclopedia of Medicine*:

"When rearing twins, especially monozygotic (single egg) twins, it is important to reinforce their importance as separate people."

Our intention in each book we write is to provide parents, children, and their teachers with words and images that will help them talk easily about a topic important to them. We hope that *About Twins* will encourage conversations about the delights, difficulties, and complexities of being a twin and, perhaps, provide new insights for the rest of us, too.

— SHEILA M. KELLY

A NOTE FROM A PARENT

Having two new babies to love and wonder about was very special to us, their parents. They knew each other first. They even spoke to each other before they learned to speak to us. We talked to other parents who had twins, and we listened to ours. We learned from them that our babies were two individual people. We saw our twins' togetherness and their need to find their own selves. And we saw them learn from each other, and from other twins, that the best part and the hardest part of being a twin is the same: You have a twin! It can be a pain, but it can also be a comfort. That's why this book is important.

AILSA McGREGOR LAUDER
Past president,
Winnipeg Parents of Twins Association

Twins are almost always born on
the same day and have the same parents.

Some twins are called identical;
they look alike.

Some twins are called fraternal;
they may look alike, or not.

Sometimes both are boys.
Sometimes both are girls.

Sometimes there's one of each.

It's special to be a twin.

Twins almost always have each other
to play with and talk to.

"Other people
might be lonely.
We hardly ever are."

Twins have to share and take turns
just like all kids.

Twins even have to share their birthday...

and their mom.

Some twins
like to dress
the same;
others don't.

"It's fun,
    but you shouldn't have to."

People always notice twins
and sometimes get them mixed up.

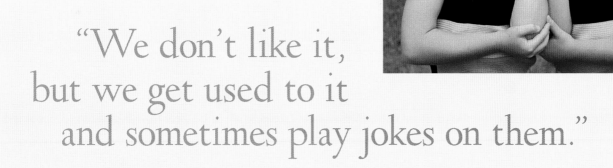

"We don't like it,
but we get used to it
and sometimes play jokes on them."

Twins don't always play together.

"It can be a pain to be a twin,
         especially if you're left out."

Twins don't always feel the same way
or like the same things.

And they can be good at different things.

"I'm really good at soccer,
and he's really good
at basketball."

Twins fight like any sisters and brothers. "Sometimes we

fight, but we make up fast so we can play."

"My twin sisters cry a lot.
When they're not around
I get a turn
with my parents."

They can make trouble,
but twins can be fun, too.

Twins are good
at taking care
of each other
and cheering
each other up.

"My twin
always
understands
me."

Sometimes a twin knows
just how the other twin feels.

Sometimes they have
the same ideas and dreams.

"One of the special things
about being a twin is that you can
usually guess what your twin is
thinking because you are together so
much of your life."

"We're twins!"

To all the parents of twins.

— SR AND SMK

DK PUBLISHING, INC.
95 MADISON AVENUE, NEW YORK, NY 10016
Visit us on the World Wide Web at http://www.dk.com

The authors would like to thank the children and parents who agreed to be interviewed and photographed for this book, especially the families from Saskatchewan. Please note that the photographs are not of the children who contributed the quotes.

Library of Congress Cataloging-in-Publication Data

Rotner, Shelley.
        About twins / by Shelley Rotner and Sheila M. Kelly ; photographs by Shelley Rotner. — 1st ed.
            p. cm.
        Summary: Examines the different kinds of twins and discusses the delights, difficulties, and complexities of being a twin.
            ISBN 0-7894-2556-4
            1. Twins—Juvenile literature. [1. Twins.] I. Kelly, Sheila M. II. Title.
HQ777.35.R69 1998   98-3060
306.875—dc21   CIP
                                                               AC

Book design by Hans Teensma / Impress, Inc.
The text of this book is set in Deepdene.

Printed and bound in the U.S.A.

First Edition, 1999

2 4 6 8 10 9 7 5 3